Irons

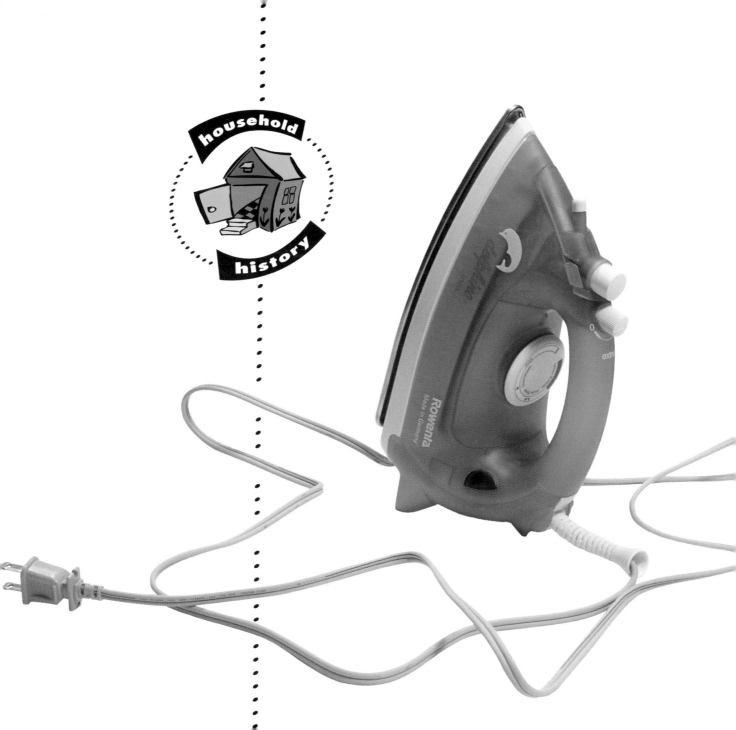

household history

Irons

Elaine Marie Alphin

Carolrhoda Books, Inc./Minneapolis

Did you spot former U.S. president Ronald Reagan on the front cover? He ironed in the 1940 film Brother Rat and a Baby.

For Art, who doesn't mind a few wrinkles as long as all the bugs are ironed out

The author wishes to thank Elizabeth Brentnall Fast Alphin for her help in providing the quotation on pages 38 and 39.

The publisher wishes to thank Jim Jurgens, Maryanne Anderson, Adell Niedorf, and Daniel R. Gospodor for their generous assistance.

Words that appear in **bold** in the text are listed in the glossary on page 46.

Carolrhoda Books, Inc., c/o The Lerner Publishing Group
241 First Avenue North, Minneapolis, MN 55401 U.S.A.
Website address: www.lernerbooks.com

Library of Congress Cataloging-in-Publication Data

Alphin, Elaine Marie.
    Irons / Elaine Marie Alphin.
      p.   cm. — (Household history)
    Includes index.
    Summary: Discusses the history and development of irons, including a brief description of how the electric steam iron works, and surveys the role of irons in popular culture.
    ISBN 1-57505-238-5
    1. Irons (Pressing)—History—Juvenile literature. 2. Laundry— Juvenile literature. [1. Irons (Pressing) History. 2. Electric irons— History. 3. Household appliances—History.] I. Title. II. Series.
TT995.A38 1998
648'.1—DC21   97–10539

Manufactured in the United States of America
1 2 3 4 5 6 – JR – 03 02 01 00 99 98

Contents

Pleats and Parasites / 6

Pressing Experiments / 14

The Iron Heats Up / 24

Beyond Wrinkles / 38

Make an Iron-on Class Quilt! / 44

Glossary / 46

Index / 48

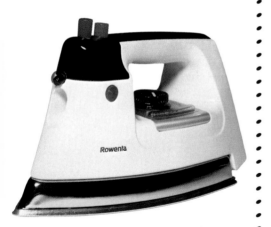

Pleats and Parasites

Baskets of fluffy laundry tumble out of the dryer. It's bad enough that kids have to match their socks and put away all the clean clothes. But parents expect more than just sorting the laundry. When you get a little older, they may expect you to pick up an **iron** and start pressing out wrinkles, too.

People have been ironing their clothes for at least 2,500 years. Why isn't it enough to wash out the mud and stains? What difference do a few wrinkles make?

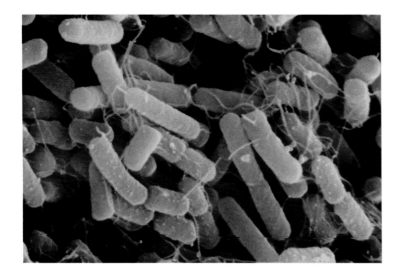

These Escherichia coli *bacteria, which are magnified 2,400 times, could show up as uninvited guests in your damp laundry.*

Whether you iron or not often depends on where you live. In some parts of the world, like the Sahara Desert, the air is dry and hot. Wet laundry dries quickly. But in other parts of the world, like the South American rain forest, the air is moist and warm. Wet laundry dries slowly. And until it is completely dry, tiny **parasites** find this moist cloth a great place to live. Flies lay their eggs in the wet laundry to provide a good home for the **maggots** that will hatch. **Bacteria** begin to form on the damp clothing. A pale coating of **mildew** can also grow on damp cloth and will spread quickly.

Iron Safety

Like all electric appliances, irons can be dangerous. Never plug in or use an iron without an adult's help. Don't touch the flat bottom of an iron, even when the iron isn't plugged in—it may still be hot. And don't use an iron near a sink or bathtub—if the iron gets wet, it could cause electric shock and even death.

Right: These women use irons filled with hot charcoal to make sure their clothing is neat and safe to wear.

Keeping a family's clothes parasite-free is hard work for this 1950s ironer.

If you hang infested clothing in a closet or put it in a drawer, then bacteria, maggots, parasites, and mildew will attack the other clothing as well. When you grab a "clean" shirt to put on, you'll brush off an insect you can see. But you can't see tiny parasites or microscopic bacteria. And when you put that shirt on, your warm body looks like an even more inviting home. Some of these critters just make you itch, but others can cause disease.

Heat and pressure can kill these bacteria, parasites, and mildew before they have a chance to settle into damp laundry. That means the clean shirt really will be clean when you put it on. So in many parts of the world, ironing is a way to keep clothing safe and healthy. In parts of southern Africa, where the climate is hot and damp, every single piece of laundry is ironed—even socks and underwear!

Since ancient times, people with enough money to hire someone (below) to do their ironing have shown off their wealth by wearing ornate clothing (left).

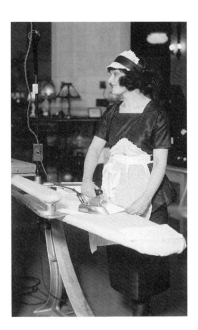

Ironing means more than cleanliness to many people, though. Wrinkle-free clothes have also been a status symbol all over the world since people began to iron. In the ancient Roman Empire, for example, only wealthy people could afford to have slaves clean and iron their clothes. And during the 1500s in Europe, only *very* wealthy people could afford to wear ruffles or pleats, which took longer to iron. In poorer families, both parents and sometimes even the children had to work to survive. No one had time to iron clothing. Fancy, wrinkle-free clothes meant that the wearer came from a family that had money.

Below: Heat in the form of electric current flows into the iron's thermostat, which adjusts the temperature. Next the current flows to the heating elements and warms the sole plate.

The Electric Exterminator

For centuries, people struggled to find a good way to iron clean clothes, both to kill parasites and bacteria and to impress others with crisp, attractive outfits. They tried glass and metal in different shapes—anything that could be heated and pressed over their laundry. Finally, in the 1880s electricity made it possible to combine heat and pressure in an electric iron.

Electric irons work by using electric power to warm a curved metal tube called a **heating element**. This heating element is coiled inside the iron, along its flat part—the **sole plate**. The sole

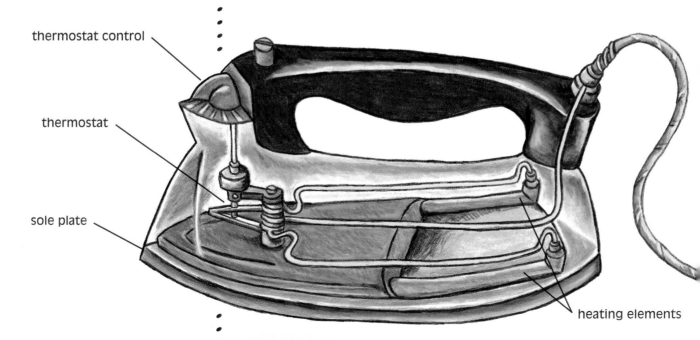

thermostat control

thermostat

sole plate

heating elements

plate is made of heat-conducting iron or steel. As the heating element grows hot, heat is transferred to the sole plate and spreads evenly across the iron or steel. When you slide the iron over a piece of clothing, the combination of heat and pressure relaxes the fibers in the fabric, which smoothes out wrinkles. The heat kills any bacteria lurking in the cloth, too.

If the heating element kept getting hotter and hotter, the sole plate would get so hot it would burn the clothing. So an electric iron has a **thermostat** (THURM-uh-stat) that controls the temperature. You can choose different heat settings, depending on what sort of fabric you are ironing. Some fabrics, like cotton, need a high setting. Others, like nylon, take a low setting. When the heating element gets too hot, the thermostat breaks the electric circuit. This removes the iron's source of heat. After the heating element cools, the thermostat reconnects the circuit. Then the heating element gets warmer once again.

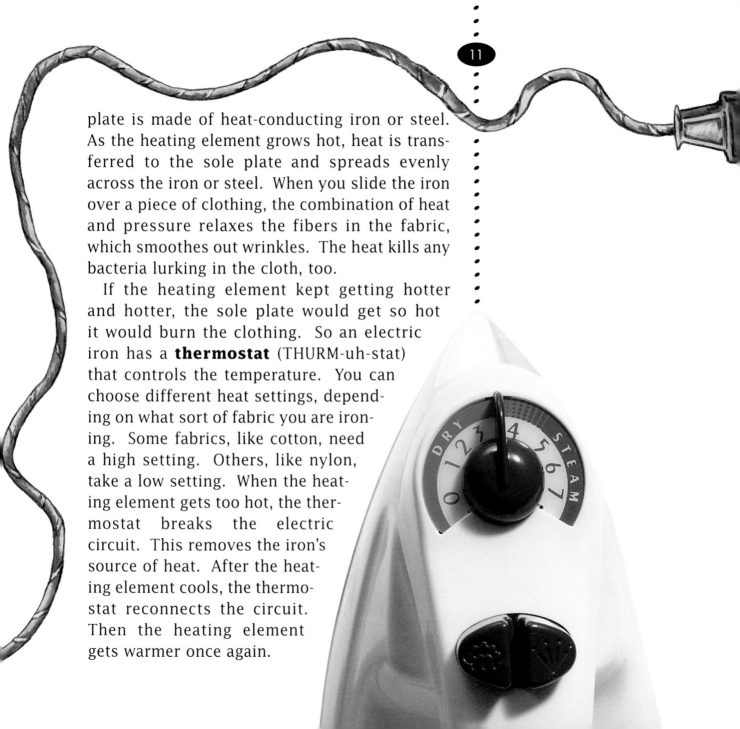

Sometimes clean clothes can be dry and stiff. It's hard to get the wrinkles out of these clothes, even with heat. In 1926 the **steam iron** became the solution to this problem. Steam irons use heated water vapor to relax the cloth fibers even more than heat and pressure can. You pour water into a small tank near the top of the iron. As the heating element warms up, the water drips from the tank onto the heated sole plate. When it lands on the plate, the water sizzles, boils, and turns to steam.

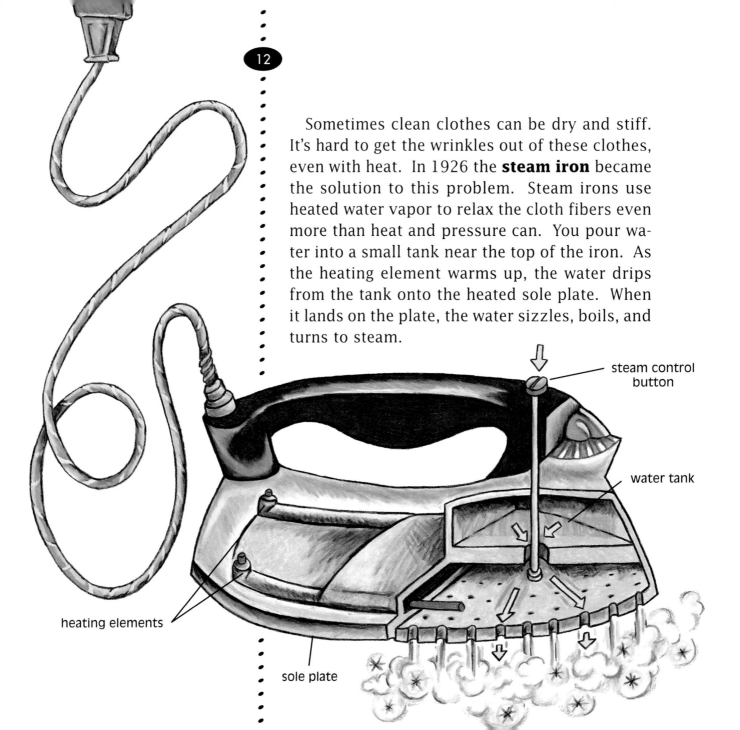

steam control button

water tank

heating elements

sole plate

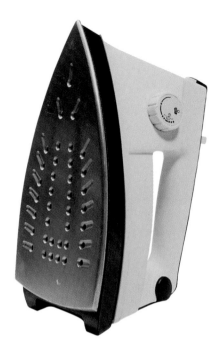

Thanks to the steam iron's holes, puffs of steam can hiss out to relax the wrinkles in your clothing. But if you try to iron before the sole plate gets hot, you'll get water, not steam—and wet laundry to go with it!

A steam iron has little holes in the bottom of the sole plate. The steam goes through these holes to the clothing. Some steam irons have a button you can push to pump out a strong gust of steam onto an especially tough wrinkle.

The electric iron makes it easier to kill bacteria that want to live in your clothes. It also makes it easier to kill wrinkles. But electricity has only been used since the 1880s. How did people iron clothes before that?

This Egyptian iron of the 1400s was heated and pressed over clothes, much like an ancient Greek goffering iron.

Pressing Experiments

Although people have been ironing clothes for at least 2,500 years, they haven't always used tools you would recognize as irons. By 400 B.C. the Greeks had invented a round bar that looked something like a rolling pin. This bar was called a **goffering** (GOFF-ur-ing) **iron.** Greek ironers heated it, then rolled it up and down their clean linen robes to press pleats into the fabric.

Two hundred years later, in 200 B.C., the Romans didn't bother with heat. They used a **hand mangle** to press their clothes. A hand mangle was a flat metal paddle. The Romans hit clothes with it to beat out the wrinkles and create pleats.

This chore wasn't something that ordinary Roman wives and children did. The Romans had slaves to do hard labor—and pressing clothes with a hand mangle was very hard labor!

By the year A.D. 800, the Chinese had invented something closer to the type of heated boxlike iron you might recognize. To make a **pan iron,** they filled a pan with hot charcoal. Then they ran the bottom of the pan across clothes to press them smooth.

The Vikings of Scandinavia used a different method in the 900s. They spread out damp clean clothes and pressed them with a **linen smoother** made of glass. This smoother looked like a mushroom. The Vikings held the smoother by its stem, then rocked it back and forth across the clothes until the wrinkles were gone and the pleats were neat.

You probably could toast marshmallows while using this Chinese pan iron—it has no lid to cover the hot charcoal.

Wealthy Europeans of the 1500s used a type of goffering iron, too. Their servants heated bar-shaped irons to make huge pleated collars called ruffs.

By the 1300s, Europeans were using a **flatiron** to press their clothes. A flatiron was just that—a flat piece of iron with a handle. The iron was held over the fire until it grew hot. Then the ironer rubbed the iron across the clothes until it cooled. Meanwhile, a fresh flatiron heated in the fire. The problem with this method was that the flatiron would get sooty from the fire, and soot made clothes dirty. To keep the clothes clean, the ironer had to place a thin cloth over them. The soot would rub from the iron onto this cloth, and only the flatiron's heat and pressure would pass through to the clothes underneath.

Soon after Europeans started using flatirons, they began to catch up to the Chinese with the **hot box.** Wealthy families owned metal irons with a hollow space inside. A servant would put heated coals, a hot brick, or a hot iron block inside the box. Then the servant could rub the iron over clean clothes to press out the wrinkles. The coals or iron block inside the hollow box might be sooty, but the iron itself stayed clean—and so did the clothes.

Dutch ironers of the 1600s had a unique problem: their country had no iron foundries and few ironworkers. So they invented hot-box irons made of brass and copper instead of iron. An actual fire, fueled by charcoal, burned inside the hot box.

In the 1780s, English artist George Morland showed a young girl using a hot box in his painting Girl Ironing.

This woman hangs her irons from a shelf above her cast-iron cookstove.

A Sad Iron

For the next 300 years, people struggled with hot boxes and sooty flatirons. Then, in the 1820s, the invention of a cookstove made of **cast iron** paved the way for new irons. This enclosed stove contained a live fire, but it burned less wood than an open fireplace and made cooking easier. It also made ironing easier. The flatirons that had carried soot to clean clothes could now be heated on a clean stove top instead.

18

French artist Edgar Degas showed what hard work sad ironing was in his 1884 painting Ironing Women. *The woman on the left sprinkles clothes with water to make them easier to press, while the woman on the right uses a heavy sad iron.*

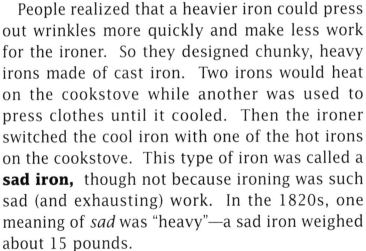

An early sad iron

People realized that a heavier iron could press out wrinkles more quickly and make less work for the ironer. So they designed chunky, heavy irons made of cast iron. Two irons would heat on the cookstove while another was used to press clothes until it cooled. Then the ironer switched the cool iron with one of the hot irons on the cookstove. This type of iron was called a **sad iron,** though not because ironing was such sad (and exhausting) work. In the 1820s, one meaning of *sad* was "heavy"—a sad iron weighed about 15 pounds.

One problem with the sad iron was that it heated unevenly. One spot might become hot enough to scorch clothes while another spot was too cool to press out wrinkles. Even worse, the handle would heat up along with the iron itself. Many ironers burned themselves because the handle was almost as hot as the bottom of the iron! Mary Potts of Ottumwa, Iowa, was an ordinary nineteen-year-old when she solved the hot-handle problem in 1870. She built a cardboard base around the body of an iron and filled it with plaster of paris. This formed a shell around the metal and kept the handle much cooler. Potts went on to develop a wooden handle that could be taken off while the sad iron was heating. The ironer reattached the handle when the iron was ready to use.

Mary Potts had no idea her iron would change the lives of ironers everywhere.

Potts's iron, with the handle detached

Above: Other companies imitated Potts's iron, but hers remained the most popular for many years.

At first Potts wasn't as good at selling irons as she was at inventing them. She went bankrupt in Iowa and nearly gave up. But Potts still believed in her sad iron, which she now called "Mrs. Potts' Cold Handle Iron." In 1876 she moved to Philadelphia, just in time for the Centennial World's Fair, where new inventions were featured. Potts's Cold Handle Iron was a hit at the Women's Pavilion at the fair and became a bestseller until the 1900s.

The Gas Explosion

Sad irons were popular and inexpensive, but the introduction of a new power source—manufactured gas—eventually meant the end of sad irons, flatirons, and hotbox irons. As early as 1816, street lamps in Baltimore were powered by gas. The gaslight system spread into homes across Europe and America, and by the 1870s nearly all major towns and cities were powered by gas. Soon irons were, too.

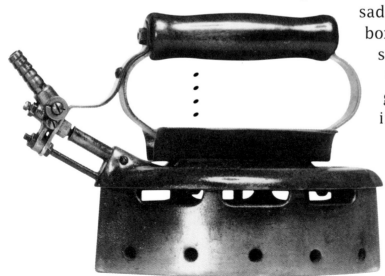

During the 1800s, many immigrants worked at difficult, dangerous jobs in sweatshops and factories. This man presses clothes with a gas iron in a New York City laundry. Behind him, another man uses a large pressing machine.

The **gas iron** actually had a fire inside. A pipe linked the iron to the gas line in the ironer's home. When this pipe was opened, gas flowed into a burner inside the iron. The ironer lit the burner with a match, and the gas fire heated the iron to a more even temperature than the old sad irons could maintain. Unfortunately, gas irons had the same hot-handle problems as sad irons.

Some irons had tanks on the back that held liquid fuel. These irons sometimes started fires and exploded.

Gas irons spared the ironer from working beside a hot cookstove.

They also leaked, ruining clean clothes. Worst of all, the gas sometimes started fires. Some gas irons even blew up!

But the lighter, sleeker gas iron seemed worth the risk to many ironers, and it was popular from the start. Gas irons were even sold by local gas companies, which were eager to offer customers more reasons for going on-line with gas. But sad irons and gas irons were still a long way from steam irons. It took electricity to create a practical way of heating an iron that was safe and easy to use.

Ironing without Irons

Inventors developed gadgets and machines that could do jobs regular irons couldn't. Fluters were heated and used to press rows of frilly pleats into collars and skirts. Ironers could also create tiny frills with heated goffering tongs, which squeezed the fabric into shape. In some laundries and garment factories, a machine called a mangle made ironing easier. The mangle had two rollers that were made of wood or metal. The ironer would lay the cloth between the heated rollers, turn a handle to roll the cloth through, and presto! Straight, flat, wrinkle-free cloth emerged in seconds.

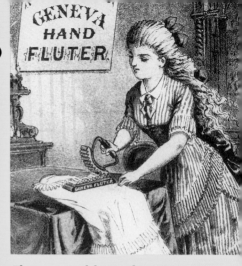

Fluters could put fancy pleats into flat, dull collars within seconds.

Mangles were usually used in professional laundries because only large businesses could afford the expensive machines.

The Iron Heats Up

An inventor named Henry W. Seely saw the possibilities of electricity first. Seely lived in New York City, where one of the first electric power stations would be built in 1882. People were already talking about using electricity instead of gas to light houses. Even before the power station had become a reality, Seely wondered what else electricity could do. He thought of an electric iron.

Seely designed a system of coils within an iron that could store the heat created by electricity.

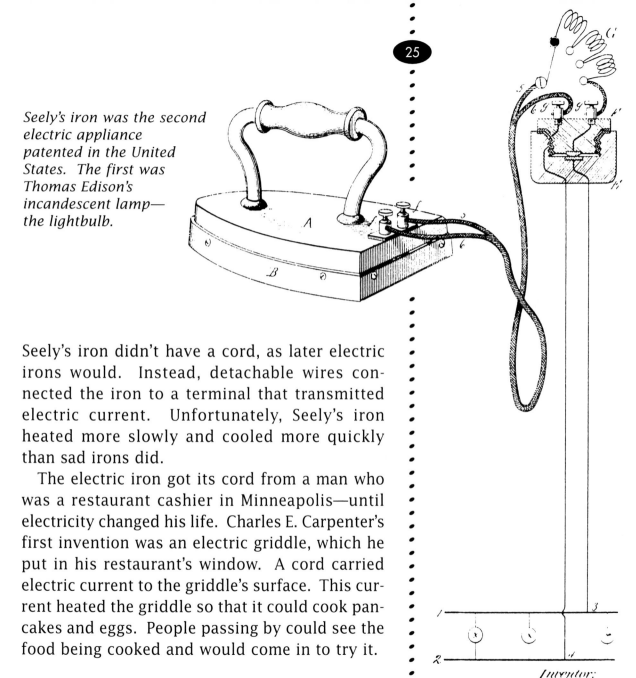

Seely's iron was the second electric appliance patented in the United States. The first was Thomas Edison's incandescent lamp— the lightbulb.

Seely's iron didn't have a cord, as later electric irons would. Instead, detachable wires connected the iron to a terminal that transmitted electric current. Unfortunately, Seely's iron heated more slowly and cooled more quickly than sad irons did.

The electric iron got its cord from a man who was a restaurant cashier in Minneapolis—until electricity changed his life. Charles E. Carpenter's first invention was an electric griddle, which he put in his restaurant's window. A cord carried electric current to the griddle's surface. This current heated the griddle so that it could cook pancakes and eggs. People passing by could see the food being cooked and would come in to try it.

Cutler-Hammer used Carpenter's technology to make irons like this one.

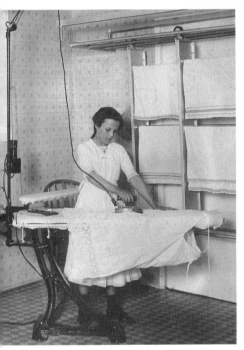

The first electric irons plugged in high on walls or ceilings, where lights were located.

One of Carpenter's friends, a tailor, asked if Carpenter could make an electric sad iron. Carpenter applied his griddle idea to the sad iron and used a cord to conduct heat directly to the iron's base. He was so pleased with the result that he moved to New York in the early 1890s and went into business. But Carpenter didn't have any experience marketing his products. In 1903 he sold his company to a manufacturer called Cutler-Hammer, which began selling his irons successfully.

Sarah Boone's Board

Although many inventors were improving the iron itself, few thought much about the surface that sat under it—the **ironing board**. During the 1800s, most people ironed on a plain wooden board wrapped with flannel. One end of the board rested on a table, the other on the back of a chair. But in 1892, an African-American woman named Sarah Boone patented a new ironing board. Boone's board featured a narrow end to make it easier to slide clothes onto the surface. It also had a wide end for linens such as sheets. By 1898 the J.R. Clark Company had built on this design and offered a collapsible ironing board with fold-up legs.

Left: Many ironers of the 1800s used hot sad irons and labored on straight, propped boards. Above: A grateful ironer enjoys a cold-handle sad iron and a collapsible board made with Sarah Boone's improved shape.

Although Seely and Carpenter invented their irons first, it was the Ward Leonard Electric Company of Wisconsin that first sold an electric iron—in 1896. Their model was a heavy electric flatiron with a cord. The iron had one drawback: its heating element didn't respond well to the intense heat the electric current supplied. It quickly wore out and stopped heating at all. Ward Leonard got around this problem by selling its iron with several extra heating elements. The weakened part of the iron could be replaced.

Richardson Makes a Point

The person who created the electric iron that is most like the one we know didn't start out as an inventor. Earl Richardson worked for the electric power company in Ontario, California. He read electric meters in Ontario homes, and he talked to housewives about electric appliances. He found that people were interested in an electric iron, but only if it were lighter and easier to use than a sad iron—and only if they could plug it in during the day.

In 1900 electric power wasn't offered to homes 24 hours a day. As with gas, this new power source was seen as a way to light homes. Power companies offered electricity only from dusk to dawn. Even if electric appliances could be invented, people would be able to use them only after dark!

Richardson tackled the weight problem first. He designed a small, lightweight, electric iron in 1903. Then he left samples of his iron with the housewives on his meter-reading route and turned his attention to daytime electricity.

Richardson had learned that most people did their ironing on Tuesdays. He figured that if people began using electric appliances, they would use more electricity. The power company would make more money. So he suggested that the company offer electricity during the day on Tuesdays only, as an experiment. The company's managers agreed to try—and were astonished by how much electricity people used. And Richardson was astonished by the requests for irons from the customers who hadn't gotten one of his original samples.

By 1905 Richardson felt confident enough about his iron that he left the power company and started the Pacific Electric Heating Company. Although the irons sold, he soon started getting complaints. The heat in Richardson's iron didn't spread evenly across the sole plate. There was a hot spot in the center, where the heating elements joined the plate. The edges of the iron were much cooler.

Earl Richardson

Richardson's first iron heated best in the center, where the rectangular heating elements met the sole plate.

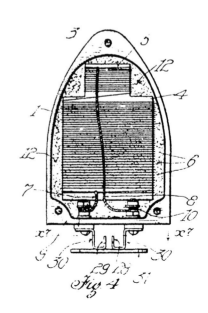

Above: This Hotpoint's cord was detachable. Below: The original Hotpoint iron

Richardson knew that the heating elements had to contact the sole plate somewhere. He asked his wife what was wrong with heating the center. She showed him that the edges of the iron, and especially the pointed tip, were more important than the center. The pointed tip nosed its way around buttons and pleats and ruffles. If the tip were cooler than the center of the iron, the ironer had to press longer to get the heat into the cloth at the buttons and pleats. That meant that the fabric under the iron's hot center might be scorched and ruined.

Richardson designed a new iron in which the heating elements met the sole plate at the tip. When he passed out samples this time, the customers were delighted. Richardson called his new success "the iron with the hot point," and in 1911 he renamed his business the Hotpoint Electric Heating Company in his iron's honor.

Competition for the Hotpoint

The American Electrical Heater Company of Detroit, Michigan, began by selling handmade electric irons to tailors, whose shops had electricity before private homes did. Robert Kuhn, one of the company's founders, knew that his irons could be a success in private households, too. He convinced the power company in Detroit not only to offer longer service hours, but also to sell irons directly!

By 1912 the American Electrical Heater Company was mass-producing the first American Beauty irons for household use. Kuhn's salesmen went door-to-door, offering their customers easy payment plans. Families could pay for an American Beauty iron with a small extra charge on their monthly electric bill. The idea took off, and over the next few decades, millions of Americans began to iron with the American Beauty.

Millions of ironers were drawn to the American Beauty's sleek, attractive design.

Frayed wrapping on early electric cords could cause fire or electrocution.

Turning Down the Heat

As electricity became more widespread and more people owned electric irons, customers asked for improvements. Inventors experimented with ways to provide even heating and increase safety. They also looked for a way to change the heat for different fabrics. Leading the search for a better iron was a teenager in Jackson, Michigan.

Fourteen-year-old Joseph Myers decided in 1912 that his mother needed an electric iron. She was impressed with it, but there was one problem. The cloth-wrapped cord ran directly inside the iron to the heating element, and the heat slowly burned through the cord. The cord would eventually fall off the iron. Even worse, the ironer could be electrocuted!

Young Myers worked in a machine shop and dreamed of becoming an inventor. He pondered the iron problem for several years. Then he took his mother's iron apart and rebuilt it with a crude automatic heat control. This switched the iron off before it got hot enough to burn through the cord. He'd solved his mother's problem, but Myers wondered if an automatic heat control could do more. Perhaps it could heat and cool the iron to keep it from scorching clothes.

Myers kept working on the design, and by 1924 he had created an iron he thought he could sell. His new heat control broke the electric circuit when the iron got too hot, then reconnected the circuit when the iron had cooled. The heat control also allowed ironers to adjust the heat for different fabrics.

As Mary Potts might have warned, marketing proved harder than inventing for Joseph Myers. It took him over a year to find the Liberty Gauge and Instrument Company of Cleveland, Ohio. Liberty tested Myers's iron by leaving it on in a basket of laundry in a fireproof room for several days. The heat control switched the iron off successfully. Impressed, Liberty launched irons based on Myers's design in 1926.

The secret to Myers's thermostat was that he used pure silver, which is very sensitive to changes in temperature.

Soon many companies produced irons with thermostats. Ironing had become easier once again.

The first steam irons had only 1 to 8 holes, but in 1952 Westinghouse offered an iron with 15. Proctor-Silex advertised 17 holes in 1958. Sunbeam went up to 36 in 1964. In 1971 Westinghouse boasted 65 holes, only to be beaten by Sears's 70 and Presto's 80. No wonder this rivalry was called a "holy war"!

Right: This early steam iron was powered by a kettle of boiling water.

Full Steam Ahead

Using water to relax wrinkles was another way of making ironing more effective. Ironers throughout history had sprinkled water or laid damp cloths on clothing. Now inventors began to wonder if they could make the electric iron dampen clothes before it pressed them. In 1926 the Eldec Company invented an electric steam iron. The handle held water that trickled down to the hot sole plate and turned to steam.

Ironers could put scented drops inside the Steam-O-Matic iron to make their clothes smell fresh.

Inventions slowed down during the Great Depression. In 1929 American business and banking systems collapsed. Many people lost their jobs, and hardly anyone had money to spend on new appliances. But inventors didn't forget about the steam iron or its major problems: leaking and rusting. Edward Schreyer of Ridgefield, Connecticut, tried a new aluminum **alloy** for the sole plate, looking for a way to make a lightweight iron that wouldn't rust. In 1938 he introduced the rustproof, leakproof Steam-O-Matic iron. It slowly heated cold water inside the body of the iron until the water turned to steam.

Irons Everywhere

Since Schreyer's success, manufacturers have built on the basic design of the electric steam iron to make the task of ironing as easy as possible. Irons feature nonstick coating on the sole plate, which makes it harder for the hot iron to stick to the fabric and scorch it. Some irons even shut themselves off if left unattended for too long. New plastics and aluminum alloys make irons lighter and easier to handle. And lightweight steam travel irons allow people to iron their clothes even on vacation.

Some companies made unusual steam irons. In 1949 the Winsted Hardware Manufacturing Company offered a steam iron with a 30-foot plastic tube that connected the iron to a water faucet. If the faucet overflowed or the tube leaked, the ironer ended up with wet laundry all over again!

Above: Nonstick coating makes ironing easier and safer than ever.

Since the 1950s, people who use electric dryers haven't had to worry about the spread of parasites and bacteria in damp clothes—the dryer's heat kills the tiny creatures. And more and more cloth manufacturers are coming out with fabrics that don't require ironing. In 1995 the same nonstick coating that protects the iron's sole plate was applied to fabrics. Clothes made from this fabric are supposed to be stainproof and wrinkleproof. Does this mean that irons are a thing of the past?

Not so fast! Other industries have borrowed the iron's design, making it useful for much more than pressing wrinkles. Manufacturers use huge heating elements, much like the industrial irons that tailors and dry cleaners use, to press and

Right: You can iron on the go with a travel iron.

seal rubber seams like the ones in your raincoat. And the automobile industry uses irons shaped like paddles to press lead or other metals into gaps between car body panels.

The computer industry has profited from improvements to the iron, too. Inventors noticed that the iron's cord often snagged against the fabric being ironed. They built an ironing board with a flexible holder called a "whip" to hold the cord above the ironing board and out of the way. In the 1990s, this whip inspired a Mouse Tamer™ that could keep a computer mouse cable from snagging papers or other objects on a desk.

Even at home, the iron has its uses outside the laundry room. Have you ever dented a piece of wooden furniture, much to your parents' dismay? Just have Mom or Dad press a damp towel over the dent and use the iron to gently steam the wood. The heat and steam relax the wood fibers the same way the iron relaxes wrinkles in your clothes. Like magic, the wood eases back into shape. And with heat-fusible webbing, which melts under heat and pressure, you can fix a rip in your favorite shirt with a touch of an iron. You could even fuse whole seams instead of hemming your pants!

The Mouse Tamer™ uses ironing board technology to keep a mouse cord out of the way.

A designer's vision of the iron of the future

William H. Johnson liked to paint pictures of his family and neighbors doing everyday things, as in this 1944 painting, Woman Ironing.

Beyond Wrinkles

You might not have to do your own ironing yet, but you probably wouldn't enjoy living without the electric steam iron. This small, hissing appliance has not only made an exhausting chore much easier, it's also changed lives. Along the way, it's become an important part of our culture, too.

Imagine what it would have been like to live during the 1800s, when sad irons were the only way to press clothes and keep them from harboring parasites and bacteria. Ironing was a chore that took a full day, every Tuesday, every week! You probably would have felt a lot like Elizabeth Brentnall, who grew up in rural Kansas before electricity was available: "I really dreaded

Tuesdays, especially in the summer. I would stand next to the sweltering cookstove which was fired up to heat the irons. Each iron would only stay hot for a few minutes. Then it had to be returned to the stove for another iron...." For women, who traditionally did most of the laundry and ironing, the invention of the electric iron had a huge impact.

The electric iron gave people a way to keep up with the laundry in greater comfort. An electric iron could be plugged in anywhere, so the ironer wasn't forced to work beside a hot cookstove.

Appliance manufacturers understood that women felt chained to their sad irons (left). When companies began to produce electric irons, they marketed them to women as a relief from drudgery. A Westinghouse ad praised the way electric irons freed the ironer from having to work next to a hot, oppressive stove. What if a woman's husband didn't want to spend his wages on an electric iron? To make sure that he got the point, Westinghouse suggested that he put a hot stove in his office and try to work next to its blazing heat.

Because the iron worked so well, the task went much more quickly. Like other household inventions, such as the vacuum cleaner and the dishwasher, the iron allowed women to take time out from housework. They could use that time to create things for pleasure, like stories or music, or to pursue an education. More women chose to work outside the home, perhaps even becoming inventors who could design tools to save others time and labor!

Spotlight on the Iron

Because of its role in improving women's lives and setting free their imaginations, the iron has become a star in our culture. Irons turn up in comedy to make us laugh almost as often as they're turned on in our homes. In the movie

Have you ever thought of an iron as a toy? How about an ironing board? In 1939 Geuder, Paschke & Frey Company advertised Met-L-Top twin ironing boards for mothers and daughters. They promised the boards would make ironing easier for Mom and fun for the kids. The twin set was even offered as a special bargain for the perfect Christmas present.

Sad ironing must have been a tough job for Peggy Ann Garner in the 1940 film A Tree Grows in Brooklyn.

This early curling iron sat in a heated tube, much like a sad iron rested on a stove.

Mr. Mom, a frustrated Michael Keaton cooks his son's grilled cheese sandwich on the ironing board with a hot iron. And in *Home Alone,* Macaulay Culkin uses the iron's flat, heavy surface to stop a burglar in his tracks.

The iron turns up in lots of other unexpected places. Sometimes people use irons not only on clothing, but also on themselves! In the 1960s, trend-setting girls thought it was cool to iron curly hair to straighten it. Have you noticed that we iron when we talk, too? If you get into an argument with a friend, the two of you try to "iron out your differences."

These sad irons are part of a treasured collection.

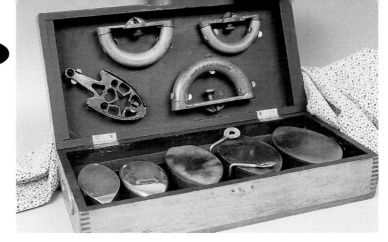

For some people, the iron isn't just a helpful appliance—it's a hobby. For serious collectors, sad irons, gas irons, and early electric irons are mementos to be displayed with pride. Does it seem strange to think of an iron cluttering up a museum cabinet? Remember the grueling work ironers faced during the 1800s. It makes sense to collect and remember the appliance that changed people's lives so much.

Because the iron can be fun as well as useful, kids benefit from it as much as adults do. Popular heat-sensitive transfers can be ironed onto your favorite clothing or a canvas book bag in only a few minutes. Some fabric paints puff up when you steam them with an iron. And you can iron leaves with waxed paper for a school science project, or try ironing grated crayons between layers of waxed paper to make a colorful "stained glass" suncatcher.

Iron-on transfers let you choose the pictures you'd like to wear.

The iron comes in handy for this ice sculptor, who uses its hot surface to attach pieces to his sculpture and smooth the edges.

One hundred years ago, you'd have spent all day Tuesday helping to iron and fold the laundry. You and your mom would be doomed to a Tuesday full of hot work, week after week after week. Next time you smooth out a shirt or a skirt for a special occasion, say a quick thanks to Mary Potts, Earl Richardson, Joseph Myers, and Edward Schreyer for helping to get the wrinkles out—and for making everyone's Tuesdays more relaxed.

Would you like to be able sit on the sofa, watch TV, and iron your clothes all at the same time? Jacques Carelman has just what you need—a remote control iron! Carelman has also invented a "wheeled iron," which rolls speedily along the ironing board to save the ironer time, and an ironing board shaped like a glove for those tough-to-press mittens.

You Will Need:

wax crayons

white copier paper or typing paper, cut into eight-inch squares

newspaper

one nine-inch square of cotton fabric per student

12 pins per student

a few needles for students to share

thread

iron

ironing board

scissors

Make an Iron-on Class Quilt!

You and your classmates can choose a quilt theme and contribute a square each to make this iron-on quilt. ***Warning****: A hot iron can cause serious burns. Try this activity only with a teacher or other adult.*

1. Choose a design for your quilt square and draw it on a square of paper. Press hard with the crayons, leaving lots of wax on the paper. If you use any letters or numbers, write them backwards.

2. Put a layer of newspaper on the ironing board. Place your quilt square on top. Lay your drawing facedown, centered on the square.

3. If you're using a steam iron, fill it with water. With your teacher's help, plug in the iron and choose the setting for cotton. Let the iron heat up, then slide it over your drawing several times, pressing hard.

4. Set the iron on the board (standing up). Let the quilt square and drawing cool, then place them on a flat surface. Slowly peel back the drawing. You'll see that the wax has melted into your quilt square.

5. When all the quilt squares are finished, turn off the iron and unplug it. Arrange the squares facedown, in rows. Your teacher can help you pin together and sew the edges of the squares in each row. Then pin together and sew the edges of the rows. Your stitches will show only from the back of the quilt.

6. You can hang the quilt in your classroom now, or finish it by sewing on a bottom layer, adding stuffing, and stitching knots where the squares meet. If the quilt gets dirty, wash it in cold water and let it air dry. Don't put it in the dryer—the heat may melt the wax and make it run.

An Iron-on T-Shirt

Make a fashion statement by ironing a design onto a T-shirt or sweatshirt (ask an adult for help). When you're ready to iron, put a piece of newspaper inside the shirt so that the crayon wax won't soak through when it melts. Center your drawing, facedown, on top of the T-shirt. Press the hot iron over your drawing. Let the shirt cool, then peel back the paper. Be sure to turn off the iron and unplug it when you're done. Make T-shirts for gifts, or try making matching shirts with a friend.

Glossary

alloy: a metal created by melting down and mixing other metals

bacteria: microscopic living things that grow quickly in a moist environment such as damp laundry

cast iron: a hard, brittle metal made by melting iron with other metals. Liquid cast iron can be poured into molds and allowed to harden to make useful objects.

flatiron: a flat piece of iron metal with a handle, heated in a fire and used to press wrinkles out of clothes and linens

gas iron: a device powered by manufactured gas and used to press wrinkles out of clothes and linens

goffering iron: a round bar of iron that looked like a rolling pin. Ancient Greeks would heat it, then roll it up and down linen robes to create crisp pleats. In the 1600s and 1700s, Europeans used a similar device, also called a goffering iron, to create frilly pleated collars called ruffs.

hand mangle: a flat metal paddle. Ancient Roman slaves hit clothes with a hand mangle to beat out wrinkles and create pleats.

heating element: a metal tube, warmed by an electric current, that transmits heat in an electric appliance

hot box: a hollow metal device that is filled with hot coals, a hot brick, or a hot metal block, then rubbed over clothing to press wrinkles out

46

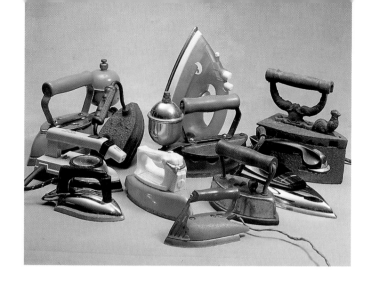

iron: a device used to press wrinkles out of clothing and linens

ironing board: a hard, flat surface on which clothing and linens are spread for pressing

linen smoother: a mushroom-shaped piece of glass that ancient Vikings used to press clothing and create pleats

maggots: the newly hatched young of flies. Some flies lay their eggs in damp laundry, spreading germs and disease.

mildew: a fungus, or plant without roots or leaves, that grows on damp cloth

pan iron: a pan filled with hot coals. The ancient Chinese rubbed pan irons over clothing to press out wrinkles.

parasites: living things that get food by living on or in other living things; in this case, tiny insects that grow on damp cloth

sad iron: a flat, heavy device made from cast iron, heated on a stove, and used to press clothes. The word *sad* meant "heavy" in the 1820s, when the sad iron became popular.

sole plate: a thin piece of steel or iron metal that forms the flat bottom surface of an electric iron

steam iron: an electric device that uses heat, pressure, and heated water vapor (steam) to remove wrinkles from clothing and linens

thermostat: this word has several meanings. In this book, it refers to a device that automatically raises or lowers the temperature in an electric iron, based on the selected setting.

47

Index

alloy, 35, 46
American Beauty iron, 31

bacteria, 7–8, 10–11, 36, 46
Boone, Sarah, 27
Brentnall, Elizabeth, 38–39

Carelman, Jacques, 43
Carpenter, Charles E., 25–26, 28
cast iron, 17, 18, 46, 47
Chinese, 15, 16, 47
cookstove, 17, 39, 40

Dutch, 16

electric iron: and safety, 7; invention of, 10, 24–35; mechanics of, 10–13, 24–35, 46, 47; social significance of, 38–40
electricity: as power source, 10–11, 22, 24, 46; availability of, 28–29, 32
Europeans, 16, 46

flatiron, 16, 17, 20, 28, 46
fluter, 23

gas iron, 20–22, 46
gas, manufactured, 20–22, 28, 46
goffering iron, 14, 46

goffering tongs, 23
Great Depression, 35
Greeks, 14, 46

hand mangle, 14–15, 46
heating element, 10–12, 28, 29–30, 36–37, 46
Home Alone, 41
hot box, 16, 46
Hotpoint iron, 30, 31

ironing: and climate, 7–8; and dirt, 16, 17; and health, 8; and kids, 6, 42, 43; and servants, 16, 39; and slaves, 9, 15, 46; and women, 39–40, 43; as status symbol, 9; hair, 41; reasons for, 6–9, 10
ironing board, 27, 37, 40, 47
iron-on transfers, 42, 44–45
irons: alternative uses for, 37, 41–42; and crafts, 42, 44–45; collecting, 42; dangers of, 7, 19, 21–22, 32; definition of, 47; history of, 6, 10, 12, 13, 14–36; in culture, 40–41; industrial uses of, 36–37; marketing of, 26, 28–30, 31, 33, 39; materials used in, 10, 14–19, 35, 46, 47; weight of, 18, 22, 28, 35, 47. *See also* electric iron *and* ironing

Kuhn, Robert, 31

linen smoother, 15, 47

maggots, 7–8, 47
mangle, 23
mildew, 7–8, 47
Mr. Mom, 41
Mrs. Potts' Cold Handle Iron, 20. *See also* Potts, Mary
Myers, Joseph, 32–33, 43

pan iron, 15, 47
parasites, 7–8, 10, 36, 47
Potts, Mary, 19–20, 43

Richardson, Earl, 28–30, 43
Romans, 9, 14–15, 46

sad iron: definition of, 47; invention of, 18–20; use of, 38–39
Schreyer, Edward, 35, 43
Seely, Henry W., 24–25, 28
sole plate, 10–12, 29–30, 47
steam iron: and safety, 7; definition of, 47; invention of, 34–35; mechanics of, 12–13, 34–35; social significance of, 38–40
Steam-O-Matic iron, 35

thermostat, 11, 32–33, 47

Vikings, 15, 47